MIGHTY MONDAY MADNESS

Coming soon to a bookstore near you:

doug & mike's Strange Kid Chronicles
Tuna Fish Tuesday
and the rest of the days of the week for that matter.

. . . but don't look for anything else because we
haven't written anything else yet. Duh.

DOUG & MIKE'S

STRANGE KID CHRONICLES

MIGHTY MONDAY MADNESS

AN

APPLE

PAPERBACK

SCHOLASTIC INC.
New York Toronto London Auckland Sydney

No part of this publication may be reproduced in whole or in part, or stored in a retrieval system, or transmitted in any form or by any means, electronic, mechanical, photocopying, recording, or otherwise, without written permission of the publisher. For information regarding permission, write to Scholastic Inc., 555 Broadway, New York, NY 10012.

ISBN 0-590-05953-X

12 11 10 9 8 7 6 5 4 3 2   8 9/9 0 1 2/0

Printed in the U.S.A.
First Scholastic printing, October 1997

For Angie

Douglas TenNapel is 6'8" tall. He created such characters as Earthworm Jim and Project Geeker. This is his first children's book.

For my two favorite girls, Liane & Kendra

Mike Koelsch is shorter than Doug. He is an illustrator and is sometimes considered a designer. When he's not making pictures he likes to surf.

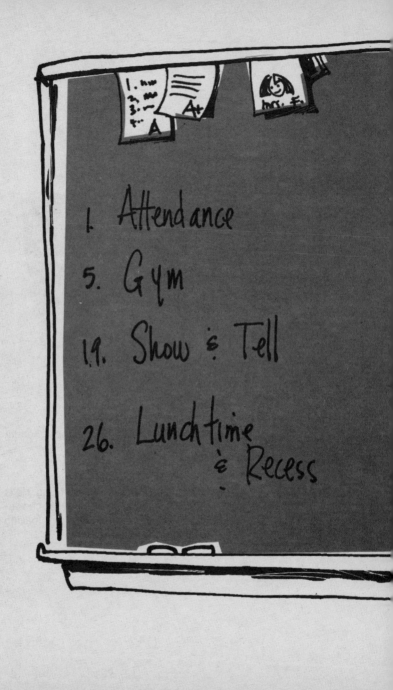

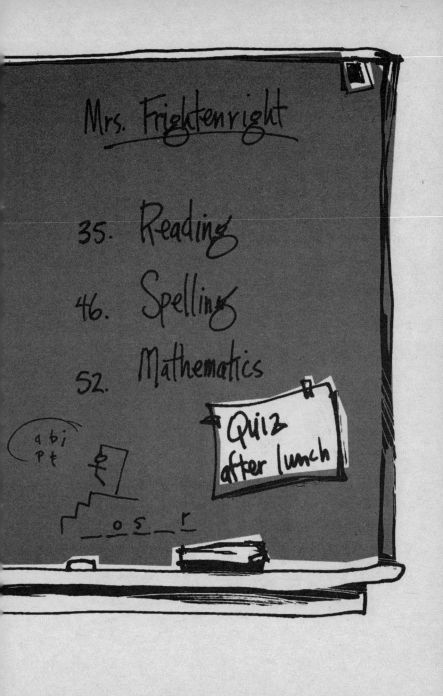

"Good golly gravy! It's Monday and the school sits in the shadow of strange things to come."

"Boy, if you get weirded out by werewolves, talking spiders, man-eating aliens, and a pig that plays backgammon, perhaps this is not the book for you."

"But if we know you . . . you're tempted . . . you're fingers start to itch . . . you can't resist and you're thinking about reaching over to grab the corner of the page . . . you must turn the page . . ."

"...Turrrrrrrn the paaaaaage!!!"

Ha!

I knew you'd do it!

ATTENDANCE

Every Monday was different in Mrs. Frightenright's class, but this particular Monday was the first day of one of the strangest weeks ever to come along in the history of education. At least that's what we think.

1

It all started that morning. Mrs. Frightenright's class lined up in front of the bike racks like soldiers. Mrs. Frightenright's class was full of . . . well . . . let's just say *different* kids. The principal peeked through his office blinds and closely watched as the kids followed Mrs. Frightenright into the school.

Principal Prickleypear was a tall thin man who wore the ugliest brown suits ever made. His eyes were beady, and he squinted every time he said the name "Mrs. Frightenright." Principal Prickleypear hated children and hated Mrs. Frightenright even more because she protected them. He watched her kids line up every day hoping someone would do something wrong so he could punish them.

But Principal Prickleypear was always let down. "Rats!" he growled under his breath. It drove Principal Prickleypear crazy knowing that everyone liked and respected Mrs. Frightenright for being such a cool teacher.

"I will give her the weirdest kids I can assemble so she will quit her job!" Prickleypear said with a sneer. "And when she leaves, her class will be mine! All mine!"

Kids exploded into the classroom. Kids slammed their locker doors. Everyone continued the morning ritual of dropping books and sharpening pencils as Mrs. Frightenright calmed the class. "Take your seats, and Willis, take that bullfrog out of your shirt and put him back in the aquarium!"

Mrs. Frightenright took attendance and collected homework while Milo played the national anthem on his harmonica. She looked across her class with pride and thanked them for settling down so quickly.

Among the kids who sat in her class was a boy named Peter Darch. He looked like a cowboy who had just got off his horse, because he walked with his legs so far apart. He had no extraordinary abilities or physical characteristics to make him special. Peter did have a normal dislike for brussels sprouts.

Last night, Glenna Darch, Peter's mother, served brussels sprouts, as she did with every meal. Whether it was stuffed chicken necks or boiled swamp oysters, Peter always found those nasty sprouts nestled beside the main course. The problem was that he could not eat the horrid vegetables if he tried.

Due to his natural distaste for this abominable food, Peter took part in the nightly ritual of stuffing all of his brussels sprouts into his pants. He gobbled down the main course, which, in last night's case, was pickled lamb's feet hash, and then went to his room with his pants full of veggies.

Today, Peter sat in the back of the class next to the hamster's cage. The hamster's name was Fang because of his large sickle-like yellow teeth. Fang loved to sink his teeth deep into anyone's hand that entered his cage. It was the thing he did best; except for eat and make little brown pellets.

Mikey Mold and Doug O'Dork, two of the slowest kids in class, once tried to arm wrestle Fang at the same time. They were both bitten so badly that they had to get stitches. To make matters worse, Fang also beat them both at arm wrestling.

Everyone was so afraid of Fang's hideous bite that his cage was rarely cleaned. A nasty stench belched forth from Fang's general vicinity, but even that was nothing compared to the odor-laden clouds that rose from Peter's pants.

Peter Darch had few friends because he smelled so bad, and after three years straight of stuffing his pants with brussels sprouts, his legs looked like giant stuffed sausages. That is all we need to know about Peter for now because it is time for gym class.

Mrs. Frightenright's class lined up double file. Everybody looked forward to gym except for Peter Darch. He hated the way his bulgy brussels-sprouts-laden pants kept him from running as fast as the other kids. And the gym teacher, Mr. Oxygen, was the meanest!

Mr. Oxygen shouted everything . . .

"HELLO PUPILS! WE ARE GOING TO DO JUMPING JACKS AND WE ARE GOING TO SWEAT! PETER, YOU WILL EXERCISE ON THE OTHER SIDE OF THE PLAY-GROUND 'CAUSE YOU **STINK**!"

 Peter dragged across the blacktop, but when he looked up, he noticed that on the other side of the playground a giant flying saucer hung in the sky. Mr. Oxygen's voice had to compete with the steady hum of the spaceship. Peter looked back at Mr. Oxygen and saw his whistle drop out of his mouth. Now Peter knew why gym teachers kept their whistles on strings--if they saw a flying saucer, their whistle wouldn't fall on the ground and get all dirty.

Big Mouth Moira saw the aircraft and screamed, "Look! A spaceship full of aliens has come to eat our brains!"

Gina Burrito said, "This is nonsense! Aliens are our friends, they will end world hunger!"

The class breathed a sigh of relief.

Big Mouth Moira saw a flashing light on the ship's antennae. "It is a death ray that will turn us into space zombies!"

The class ran behind Mr. Oxygen as his hulking torso stuck out bravely before the ship.

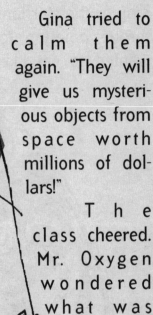

Gina tried to calm them again. "They will give us mysterious objects from space worth millions of dollars!"

The class cheered. Mr. Oxygen wondered what was inside this floating vehicle of mysterious origin.

The ship housed a hostile creature from the planet Mars who had come to take over the United States. His name was Jerry, King of the Martians, and he sat on a mighty throne pointing to the people whom he wanted to eat like candy. Jerry had three

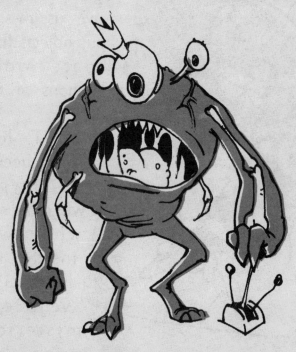

large eyes about the size of grapefruits. Jerry's skin was transparent, so you could see his skeleton through his disgusting green flesh.

As soon as the bug-eyed ruler saw Peter, his giant, orange, zit-covered tongue flopped out of his mouth and he drooled like a dog in a butcher's shop. So a giant stalk with a mechanical claw dropped down from the belly of the ship and clutched Peter, who was about to be the king's next meal. Mr. Oxygen tried to grab Peter away from the claw, but his hands slipped off the slimy brussels-sprouts-filled pants. Peter was so scared that he passed out.

Peter woke up served on a plate, parsley garnish in his mouth, and set up in front of the King of Martians. Peter was feeling uncomfortably soggy when he noticed that the spacecraft was full of metallic gizmos that sprayed a fine mist to keep the King of Martians moist. But he didn't mind the wetness. Rather, he was relieved that at least he was not being served with a side dish of brussels sprouts. Instead, Peter lay next to a family of gooey slugs who had obviously realized they were about to be eaten.

"Please, help us!" begged Poppa gooey slug. (Peter figured he was the father due to his mustache.) "How can I help when I am tied up?" Peter said.

"I don't suppose you can help us," the father gooey slug said. "And by the way . . .

"YOU STINK!"

Peter was going to roll over and crush the gooey father slug when the Martian King pulled his chair up to the table and started to eyeball Peter. And with three eyes, he was *really* good at it! Peter tried to make the best of his situation. "Hello Mr. Alien, you must be here to end world hunger!"

The Martian King just licked his lips and sprinkled salt all over Peter.

Peter cleared his throat and said, "Um, you must be here to give us mysterious objects from outer space worth millions of dollars!"

The Martian King replied, "We have come to eat your brains and shoot you with a death ray that will turn you into a zombie!"

Peter realized that he was doomed.

"After I am done eating your legs," the king said, "I will eat your nose, then your head!"

The veins on the alien emperor's head pulsed with delight as he bit down on Peter's pant leg. Peter unbuttoned his pants and willingly let the creature munch away at the trousers' disgusting contents, knowing that

the King of Martians was in for a surprise.

Just when the King of Martians was about to threaten Peter again, a great mass of rotten brussels sprouts slid down his throat. His third eye exploded as Peter escaped. The taste of brussels sprouts was so bad that the alien fell dead. Peter scooped up the family of gooey slugs and put them in the driver's seat of the flying saucer. The slugs then lowered the ship's claw so Peter could slide back down to the ground.

Peter safely landed next to Mr. Oxygen and his admiring classmates. As the gooey slugs drove the flying saucer back into space, Mr. Oxygen patted Peter on the back.

"Peter, you're a hero," he said.

"Thank you, sir," Peter answered.

Mr. Oxygen laughed. "A hero without any pants!"

Peter Darch's face turned red when he realized that he was standing there in his underwear.

Gym was over, and the kids hurried back to Mrs. Frightenright's class.

Mrs. Frightenright handed Peter a large blanket so he could cover up. "Peter was so brave!" the class said as they told Mrs. Frightenright the whole story. Peter was just happy to be wearing a blanket!

Glenna Darch was so proud of her son that later that evening she rewarded Peter with any dinner the boy wanted.

"I would like stuffed chicken necks!" Peter said.

His mother asked, "What would you like to eat with them?"

"Carrots!" Peter answered.

Mrs. Darch set a dinner plate in front of Peter full of hot, steaming, stuffed chicken necks with a side of cooked carrots. Peter did not like the look of the carrots. He did not like the look of them at all.

Peter stuffed the carrots into his pants.

SHOW & TELL

Mrs. Frightenright continued with her schedule. "It is time for someone to share with us what they did this summer! Any volunteers for show-and-tell?"

No *one* dared raise *their* hand except Big Mouth Moira. She *always* raised her hand because she loved to talk. Moira was a frightening sight to most, but she didn't care. She already had a best friend, a pig named Jared who she took everywhere she went. Jared, who had a pretty big mouth too, thought Moira was a wonderful girl and admitted that she was the only person who could beat him at backgammon.

Big Mouth Moira strutted to the front of the class holding Jared's hand. She opened her mouth wide and began her story.

"On sunny days, Jared and I like to take long walks on the beach. I can open my mouth as far as it will go when I talk at the beach, since there is so much room."

Truman turned and whispered to Gina Burrito, "Look at the colossal size of Moira's mouth!"

Gina giggled. "You could park the school bus in that mouth and lift the hood with plenty of room to spare!"

Moira ignored the whispering and continued with her story. "On this one hot day, the beach was crowded with people who came from miles around to swim and get eaten by sharks. Then I heard a loud rumble coming from the ocean. It sounded like this:

RUMBLE RUMBLE WHOOSH!

I didn't see what it was at first, because I was busy setting up another backgammon game and spreading tanning oil on Jared. My little piggy pal was so shiny that he was like a mirror, and when I looked at the reflection on his belly I saw it . . . it was the biggest tidal wave ever to hit the coast of California. The gargantuan wave was filled with hundreds of sharks, a few kelp beds, a giant squid, and one tiny little tuna. By the time we saw the tsunami, there was only one thing we could do to save thousands of people. "You see, I know I have a slightly larger mouth than some . . ."

Skeleton Joe whispered, "Yeah, and Earth is slightly larger than a gumball!"

Big Mouth Moira glared at Skeleton Joe for a second, then continued. ". . . but even my mouth wasn't huge enough to stop a tidal wave. Then I got an idea from a nature show I once saw where a big snake unhinged its jaws to swallow a rabbit twice its size. Jared and I unhinged our jaws, which allowed us to open our mouths so wide that you could park a bus . . ."

"A school bus!" Gina shouted.

". . . you could park

a school bus

inside and open

the hood

with plenty of

room to spare.

Big Mouth Moira pulled out a shiny gold key from her pocket and a newspaper article that proved her story beyond a doubt. **"This key to the city is the mayor's highest honor, awarded to Jared and me."**

Mrs. Frightenright asked, "Jared, what did you do with

all of that water in your tummy?"

Jared snorted, "Man, I must have peed for a --"

"Thank you, Moira and Jared, you may be seated!" Mrs. Frightenright interrupted.

LUNCHTIME & RECESS

Weird Ellis sat in the back of the classroom trying to have a staring contest with his sock puppet. The puppet's eyes were made of two shiny black buttons that Weird Ellis had sewn to one of his socks the night before. Weird Ellis rubbed his eyes and screamed,

"Rats! You win again!"

Just as Weird Ellis got upset, Mrs. Frightenright dismissed the class for lunch. Ellis did not eat in the cafeteria with the other kids. He got the creeps from Helga, the milk lady. "She passes out the cartons of milk just before you pass out from looking at her horrid brown teeth." The kids all agreed.

Ellis's stomach growled, "Meee hungry!"

At last, the bell rang. "Lunch is over! RECESS . . . finally!" Weird Ellis whispered to himself. Mrs. Frightenright dismissed the class. All of the kids shot out of the cafeteria like cannonballs.

Weird Ellis ran to his favorite swing that hung from an old elm tree at the far end of the playground. Every day, crows the size of dogs brought Weird Ellis snacks in trade for a story.

"Once upon a time," he began, "there was a scarecrow!"

All of the crows gasped in fear.

"Oh, man, I hate those things!" one crow said.

Another crow asked, "Weird Ellis, is this going to be another scary story?"

Then the first crow said, "I don't want to hear another scary story. I want my sandwich back!"

Weird Ellis did not want to give up his squid-butter-and-garbanzo-bean sandwich, so he quickly changed his story. "Did I tell you

that this scarecrow was not the least bit scary?"

The crows were interested in his story once again. "Tell us more. Why was this scarecrow not scary?" they asked.

"He was not scary because he wore a dress!" Weird Ellis answered, and they all laughed. He finished his story and his snacks, then said good-bye to his feathered friends.

The smallest crow asked, "What's your hurry, Ellis? Ain't you gonna show us your **Weird Eye**?"

Weird Ellis answered, "Every time I come out here you guys ask me to show you my **Weird Eye**, and every time I show my **Weird Eye** you fellas just laugh at me!"

The biggest crow hopped forward and said, "We won't laugh this time, Ellis. We know that it is a sacred ritual that your grandpa taught you and should not be laughed at!"

Ellis gave in and agreed to show his **Weird Eye**. Taking a deep breath, he concentrated very hard and covered his eyes with his hands. Within a few seconds a giant eyeball, the size of a car tire, appeared over his head, wobbly at first, fading in and out until it stabilized. Finally the giant eye floated above Ellis's head, and the crows just stared at it, smiling.

One crow snickered. Then the little one guffawed. There were a few moments of silence, until all the crows roared with laughter. Ellis removed his hands from his eyes and the **Weird Eye** disappeared. Ellis was furious! He stormed off as the crows continued to laugh. "Man, did you see the size of that eye? Next time we should poke it and see what happens!"

Ellis mumbled to himself, "Stupid birds! Why if it wasn't for them bringing me lunch every day I'd--"

Ellis heard a commotion coming from Mrs. Frightenright's class. He stepped into the classroom and saw a scary phantom appear just in front of the chalkboard. This phantom was bluish with a top hat, tie, and mustache. He threw books at Doug O'Dork, which made a hollow sound when they struck his head and he passed out. Mrs. Frightenright was so scared that her hair jumped off her head and ran into the boys' bathroom. Some kids screamed. Others ran out of the classroom. But not Weird Ellis. His grandpa taught him what to do if he ever saw a phantom.

Weird Ellis knew that the giant eyeball was not scary to crows or people. But it was scary to phantoms. He walked right up to the phantom and said, "Specter, you don't scare me!" Then he covered his eyes in preparation to give this ghost guy the **Weird Eye**. The giant eyeball appeared over his head. The phantom was so scared that he wet his sheet. "I'm so embarrassed!" the phantom cried, looking down at his soaked sheet. He then floated though the ceiling, leaving only a ghostly top hat behind.

"Don't come back," said Weird Ellis, "or you'll get the **Weird Eye** again!"

Bald Mrs. Frightenright thanked Weird Ellis, and she noticed his cool new hat that he wore with pride.

REaDING

Mrs. Frightenright prompted the class to open their textbooks and prepare to take turns reading stories. She called on Gina Burrito to read first. Gina Burrito was your basic kid, except for her amazing power to turn herself into a burrito anytime she wanted. She never showed this ability to any of her classmates because she did not want them to make fun of her, or worse -- to take a bite out of her.

Nobody noticed that when Gina Burrito's shadow cast across the classroom, it made the shape of a burrito instead of the

shape of a little girl. Gina Burrito's special ability, to turn into a burrito, remained a secret until this day. The werewolves paid a surprise visit to Mrs. Frightenright's class.

Yes, that's right! Werewolves! Three of

them! Just when Gina was about to start reading, they came through the window and stole the goodies out of the students' snack bags. Their fangs were so big that Gina thought they were horns growing out of their mouths. **Their breath was repulsive like curdled milk,** and a **frothy rabies-infested lather** oozed off their lower jaws.

The smallest beast took a Chocolate-Wing-Ding-Thing from Weird Ellis's snack bag. The big blue were-wolf turned Mrs. Frightenright upside down by her ankles, hoping to shake a stick of gum out of her pocket. Jared the pig then reached for his backgammon board and whacked the big blue werewolf on his head. The wolf wearing braces ate a chunk of fudge and then sniffed the air and said,

"I smell Mexican food!"

Brace Face followed Gina's spicy Mexican food smell right to her desk!

"I believe I smell a burrito!"

he decided, licking his chops. It is a documented fact that werewolves are Mexican food experts. They can smell a pinto bean

from over a mile away. In fact, one
werewolf in Texas tracked the scent
of an unopened jar of salsa in a

fireproof safe!

Gina Burrito knew that she was in danger, so she dropped her reading book, jumped up onto Fang the hamster's cage, and pulled the little rodent out. Gina knew to hold him by the tail because that rascal did like to bite. Now the werewolf could smell only hamster, and not Gina Burrito.

Fang bared his fangs and tried to bite Gina's hand. Gina tossed Fang to the werewolf wearing braces. He gobbled up the hamster as Gina Burrito ran for the door.

All three wolves, Mrs. Frightenright, and the rest of the classroom were amazed as . . .

Gina...

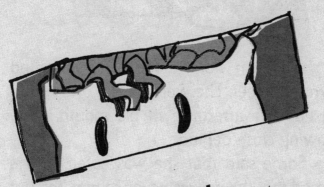

...turned into...

...a burrito.

Gina ran out of the classroom and down the street. The werewolves, one with a bad hamster aftertaste in his mouth, were following close behind.

Some said that she was eaten, others claimed that the wolves never caught her, but neither Gina nor the werewolves were ever seen again.

Many months after this incident, a mysterious postcard came to Mrs. Frightenright's class that said:

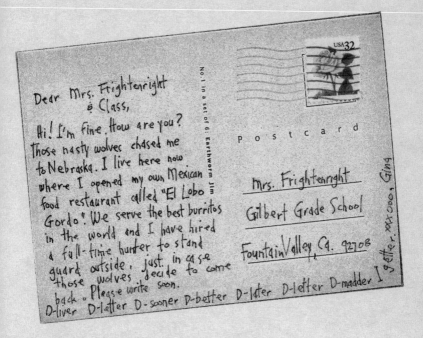

Dear Mrs. Frightenright & Class,

Hi! I'm fine. How are you? Those nasty wolves chased me to Nebraska. I live here now where I opened my own Mexican food restaurant called "El Lobo Gordo". We serve the best burritos in the world and I have hired a full-time hunter to stand guard outside, just in case those wolves decide to come back. Please write soon.

D-liver D-letter D-sooner D-better D-later D-letter D-madder I getter. xxx ooo, Gina

No. 1 in a set of 6: Earthworm Jim

USA 32

postcard

Mrs. Frightenright

Gilbert Grade School

Fountain Valley, Ca. 92708

Mrs. Frightenright and all the kids in class wrote Gina Burrito letters thanking her for being so courageous. They also sent her drawings and candy. Here are some of the dawings and letters:

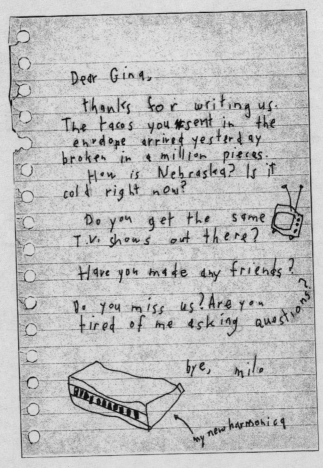

Dear Gina,

thanks for writing us. The tacos you sent in the envdope arrived yesterday broken in a million pieces.

How is Nebraska? Is it cold right now?

Do you get the same T.V. shows out there?

Have you made any friends?

Do you miss us? Are you tired of me asking questions?

bye, milo

my new harmonica

Dear Gina Burrito,

I thought of a great way for us to make money. Can you turn yourself into a solid gold burrito? If so give me a call and we can be rich!

Carlos

SPELLING

Mrs. Frightenright fanned her face with an envelope, trying to cool down. "Well, that was exciting. Any comments or questions from the class?" Mrs. Frightenright looked around for any raised hands. There were no raised hands, but there were lots of staring eyes! The kids could not stop looking at her.

"Good. Since it is the beginning of the week, we have a new spelling list to study." She saw that all of the students were staring at her bald head, so she asked, "Did anyone see where my hair went?"

Milo answered, "I think I saw it run into the boys' bathroom!"

Mrs. Frightenright asked, "Would you be so kind as to bring it back to me?"

Milo gladly volunteered.

Milo was only five years old, but the greatest harmonica player who ever existed. Milo played harmonica in the morning, he played harmonica at lunch while he ate, he played at dismissal, and he even played harmonica at dinner because his parents let him. In fact, because he was so good at playing the harmonica, he got moved up three grades! So he was the youngest member in Mrs. Frightenright's class.

Milo entered the bathroom and found Mrs. Frightenright's hair cowering in the corner next to the trash can. Milo picked it up,

put it in his pocket, and was about to leave the restroom when in walked Big Bully Rusty. It was said that Big Bully Rusty was twenty years old and still in the third grade. This is because he had been held back so many times. Big Bully Rusty was covered with hundreds of fleas and he scratched himself like a dog. It was also kind of weird that he buried bones in his backyard. Big Bully Rusty grabbed Milo's harmonica and flushed it down the toilet. It was clear that little Milo was very sad, so Rusty asked,

"What are you going to do, Milo, cry to your momma?"

Milo said, "No, I'm going to feed you to my

giant scorpion."

MATHEMATICS

Milo came back to class and gave Mrs. Frightenright her hair, and she carefully placed it back on her head. She gave Milo a spelling list and turned to the class. "Let's get our math books out and turn to page three hundred and fifty-one."

Most of the students hated math except Carla Medulla, the world's smartest kid. Mrs. Frightenright patiently went over the lesson and warned that a quiz could pop up at any time.

Principal Prickleypear entered the class holding a clipboard. He seemed to be watching every move Mrs. Frightenright made. Spider-Speaking Spencer sat in his chair holding a pencil with a big fat spider swinging on the eraser. Principal Prickleypear hated spiders. He shivered, rolled his eyes, and mumbled to himself, "Maniacs! The whole class!" as he left the room.

Mrs. Frightenright looked at the clock. There was

still a half hour before dismissal, which was plenty of time for a quiz. Mrs. Frightenright announced, "It is time to put your books away, get out your pencils, and take a math quiz. And no peeking, Eyeball Smith!"

Eyeball Smith was a kid with fifty eyes stuck all over his head. At first he was thought to be as smart as Carla Medulla. But then it was revealed that he was just copying her answers even though she sat directly behind him.

Mrs. Frightenright went to reach for the pile of quizzes. She noticed a few spider-webs growing on her desk that she had not seen before. Then, as she looked around some more, Mrs. Frightenright noticed that the entire classroom was rapidly being covered in tiny white threads. In fact, with

every second that passed, the threads grew in

number. A few minutes later, the entire room

was encased in a cocoon!

The children grew uneasy as spooky

webs covered every surface in the room.

Doug O'Dork stood up and said, "Mrs. Frightenright, my desk is so covered in webbing that I can't find my pencil!"

Milo answered, "It's stuck to your cheek, weirdo!"

It was true. The pencil had been webbed to Doug's cheek. Mikey Mold held up a pair of scissors. **"I'll cut it off!"**

"No!" Mrs. Frightenright yelled. "The math quiz is **canceled!**"

Mrs. Frightenright figured that since it was so late in the lesson, her class could have fun at the playground for the last fifteen minutes of the day.

The kids cheered, "Hooray! Hooray! Hooray!

No math quiz!"

"Gather your things for dismissal," Mrs. Frightenright instructed.

Everyone brushed spiderwebs off their personal belongings and prepared to leave. Moira spit on a tissue and wiped Jared's face like somebody's mom saying, "Icky! Icky webs!"

Within a few minutes the classroom was empty, with one exception -- Spider-Speaking Spencer. He was still in his chair talking to the tiny spider perched on his pencil. Spencer said to the spider, "Nice job. I think we need some more on the ceiling."

It is well known that Spencer talks to spiders. If there was ever a dank, dirty corner filled with spiderwebs. Spence was there crouching, talking to them.

"Hey, Spence!" the spider on his thumb said, "remember your promise. I get my pals to web up the class to get you out of your math quiz, and in return you feed me a

big fat cricket!"

Spencer reached into his ear and pulled out a fat brown cricket. "Here you go, Mr. Spider," Spencer said.

Mr. Spider strapped the cricket to his back. "Now what about my pals?"

"I'll feed them, too!" Spencer answered.

Mr. Spider smiled, then hopped away.

Spencer walked back into the heart of the webbing under Mrs. Frightenright's desk and opened up his coat pocket. Hundreds of fat brown crickets poured out as the hard working spiders came to fetch their reward.

The spiders then set up a bunch of tiny tables and chairs and announced a feast in Spencer's honor. The little guy spiders put on party hats and tuxedos, while the little women spiders wore beautiful gowns covered with diamonds.

While eating, they sang wonderful songs about **Spencer:**

We'll suck out the eyes!
This feast is a miracle!
We'll bake them in pies,
and eat up their spiracles!

Spencer made the spiders fat and happy.

One of the old fat spiders stood on top of a number two pencil and addressed the crowd of arachnids. He opened his mandibles and spoke, "As all of you know, Spencer has been our friend for a very long time. He has fed us so well today that I arranged a surprise for him! Follow me, everybody!"

Spencer was led to a giant throne made of spiderwebs. The old fat spider said, "Spencer, because you have shown us such kindness we would like you to be our king."

Spencer's mouth dropped open, for he knew that no other human had ever received so high an honor in the Kingdom of the Spiders. Spencer slowly sat in the soft, comfortable throne. They made him a big

spider-shaped crown that he wore
with dignity and purpose.

Then a strange thing happened.

Every spider in the world, billions of
them at the same time, bowed down
for a few seconds to honor Spencer.
The classroom door burst open and
Principal Prickleypear stormed in with
the janitor.

"Clean up this mess right away! Werewolves, ghost,spaceships, and now cobwebs! The school board will hear about this and Mrs. Frightenright will be fired!"

The janitor said, "I think the kids like this stuff. Everyone knows that Mrs. Frightenright is the best teacher you've got!"

Principal Prickleypear wrapped an evil smile around his head and hissed, "Is she ever in for a surprise when she sees the student I'm bringing to her class tomorrow!"

Spencer watched Prickleypear slink out of the room as the janitor cleaned the cobwebs with a broom. He was careful to let the spiders scurry back into the cracks where they came from so that only their webs were thrown in the trash.

Spencer knew that the party couldn't last forever. But it was still and would always be the greatest day in Spencer's life. After all, it was official now . . . he was the

Spider King.

While out on the playground the class heard the school dismissal bell ring. The buses came, the children left, and Mrs. Frightenright noticed that Principal Prickleypear was spying on her from outside. She knew he was up to something. Perhaps tomorrow would shed some light on his strange behavior. She looked at her pocket calendar to see what was scheduled for Tuesday.

"Oh my! It will be an interesting day!" she said as she stepped into her hot rod to drive home.

Mikey Mold and Doug O'Dork began their long walk home.

Mikey Mold said, "Man, what a crazy-whacked day!"

"What kind of funky things will happen tomorrow?" Doug wondered.

Mikey answered, "You never know in Mrs. Frightenright's class . . . probably **giant ants** or something."

Doug laughed. "**Giant ants**. You're nuts!"

"How about **giant uncles**?" Mikey said.

Beware, for tomorrow is
Tuesday!

Are you scared of what that day will bring? Well, you should be! Here's a peek at what's in store for Mrs. Frightenright's class . . .

See **you** in class tomorrow!